CW00328163

CHESTER'S EASIEST
RAGS

by Carol Barratt

1. Ragtime
2. Rag Day
3. Racoon Rag
4. Rainy Day Rag
5. Peanut Rag
6. Rag-and-Bone March
7. Sad Rag
8. Alabama Rag
9. Ragamuffin
10. Rag-Fair
11. Ragmobile
12. Tyrolean Rag
13. Ragtime Waltz
14. Rickety Rag
15. D-I-Y RAG

Exclusive distributors:

Music Sales Limited
8/9 Frith Street, London
W1V 5TZ, England

Music Sales Corporation Distribution Center,
257 Park Avenue South
New York NY10010,
U.S.A

Music Sales Pty Limited,
120 Rothschild Avenue,
Rosebery, NSW 2018
Australia.

This book © Copyright 1990 by
Chester Music Limited
UK ISBN 0.7119.2276.4
Order No. CH 58727

Art direction by Mike Bell
Cover illustration by Sarah Lenton
Music processed by Barnes Music Engraving Limited
Printed by Caligraving Limited, Thetford, Norfolk.

Chester Music Limited
(A division of Music Sales Limited)

£4

FOR SUPER SYNCOPATION

Knees can be very useful! To help you get to grips with syncopation, try tapping out these exercises **slowly** before tackling the relevant pieces. (Don't hurt yourself when you see > !)

For Pieces 1 and 2

For Pieces 3 and 4

For Pieces 5 and 6

For Pieces 7 and 8

(Pieces 9, 10 and 11 – easy rhythms)

For Piece 12

For Piece 13

For Piece 14

For Issie Barratt

CHESTER'S EASIEST RAGS is a really easy introduction to
an early jazz style called **ragtime-** a piece of music in this style
is called a **rag.**

Ragtime grew out of black-American (Afro-American) music
and was extremely popular as dance music around 1900.
Ragtime rhythms are very syncopated, and piano rags were
often described as "playing two different times at once".

In this book, five-finger hand positions gradually lead into
a more extended range, and

the syncopation develops from ♩ ♩ ♩ to ♫♩♫♩.

Everyone loves to play rags, so get practising and enjoy yourself.

Carol Barratt

1.
RAGTIME

Scott Joplin—the King of Piano Rags—often wrote the following words above his music:

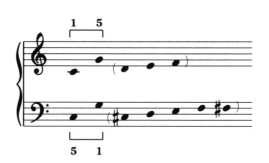

Notice! Don't play this piece fast. It is never right to play 'rag-time' fast.

With a steady beat

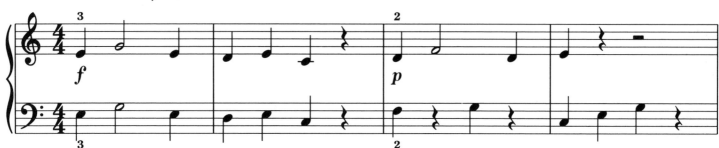

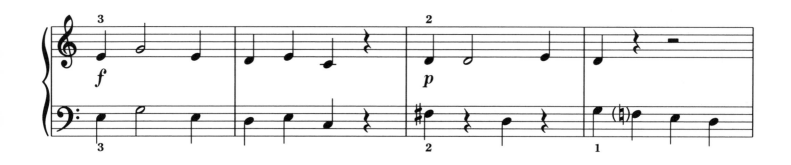

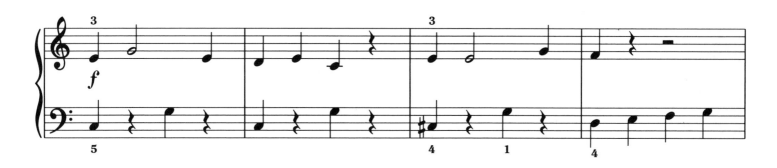

© Copyright 1990 Chester Music Limited. CH 58727 All rights reserved

2.
RAG DAY

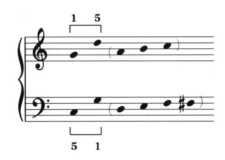

Slowly, but with spirit

3.
RACOON RAG

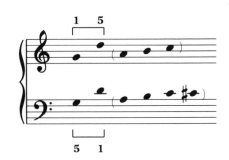

Not fast

4.
RAINY DAY RAG

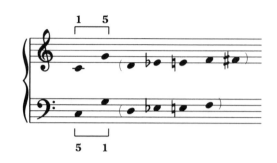

5.
PEANUT RAG

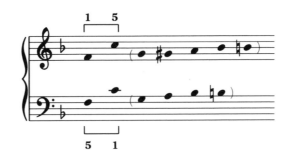

6.
RAG-AND-BONE MARCH

7.
SAD RAG

8.
ALABAMA RAG

9.
RAGAMUFFIN

Set 5 finger Hand Positions will not necessarily be used from now on.

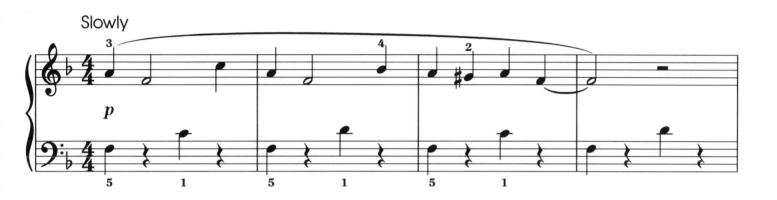

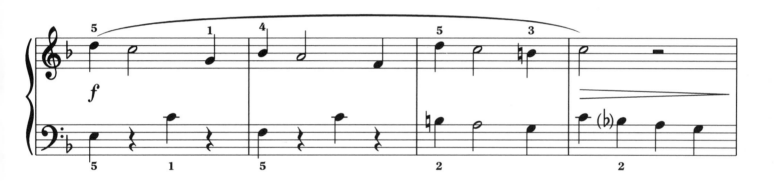

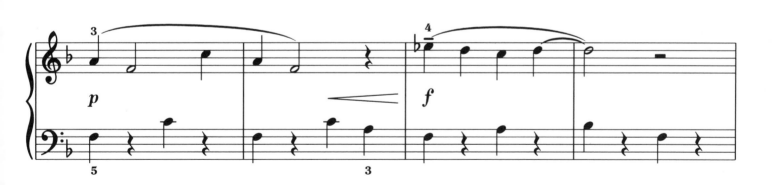

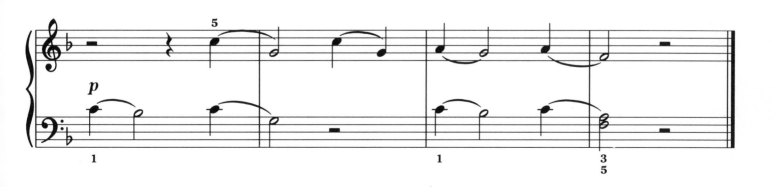

10.
RAG-FAIR

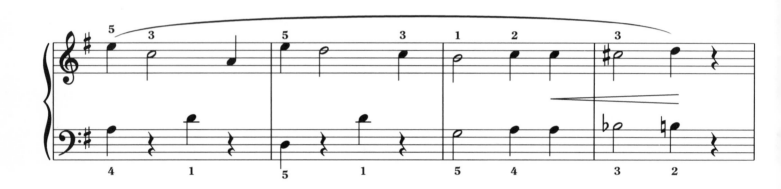

11.
RAGMOBILE

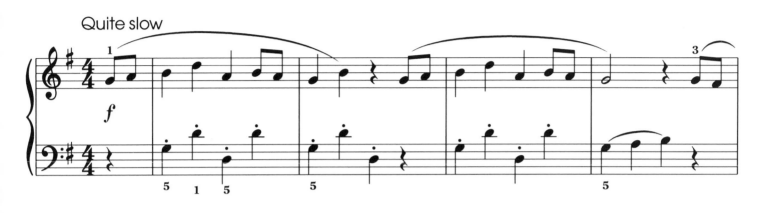

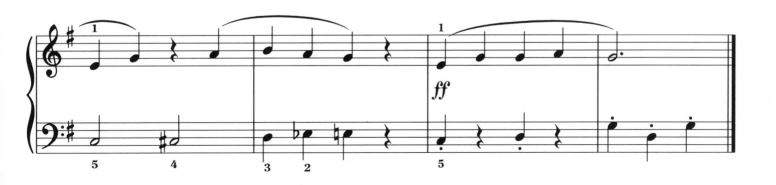

12.
TYROLEAN RAG

13.
RAGTIME WALTZ

Slow, lazy beat

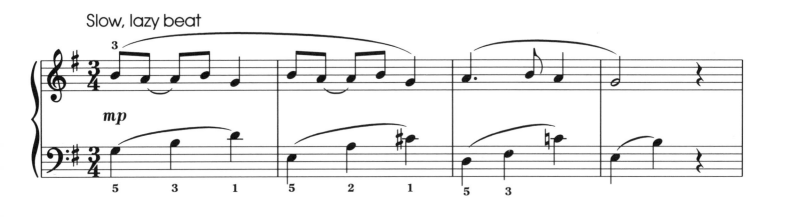

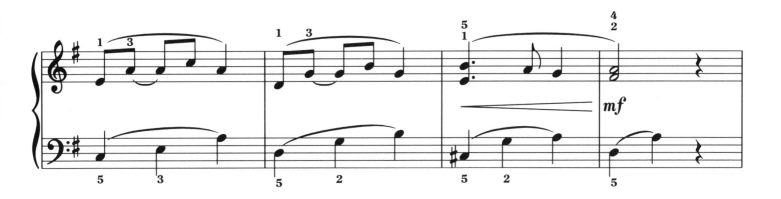

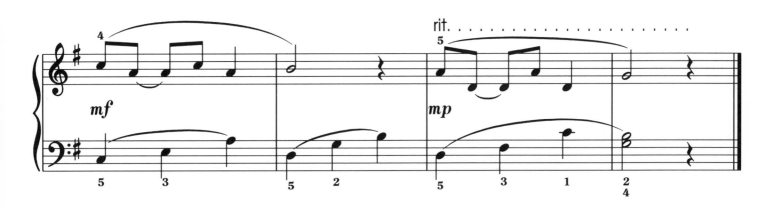

14.
RICKETY RAG

Slowly, but with spirit

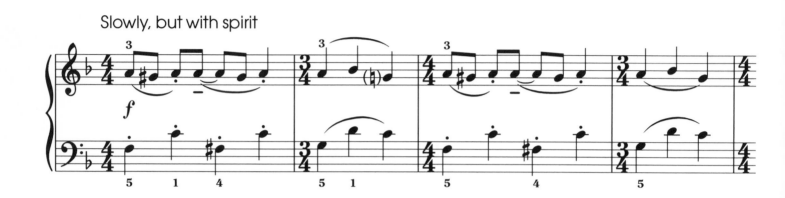

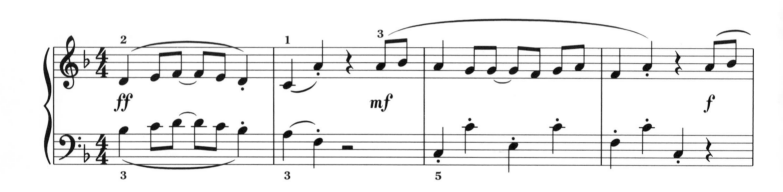

15.
D-I-Y RAG

Go on! Write your own rag. The Left Hand part has already been written for you. (It is taken from piece number 2 – 'Rag Day.')

Suggested range for the Right Hand.

Slowly, but with spirit

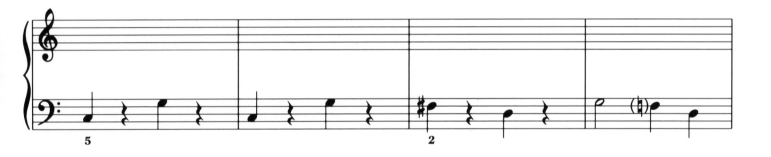

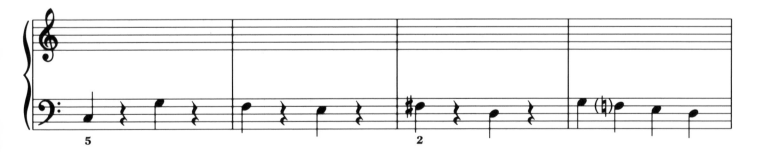